Disney's
DOUG
Created by
Jim Jinkins

The Funnie
MYSTERIES

The Curse of Beetenkaumun

by Pamela Pollack

Illustrated by William Presing

The Curse of Beetenkaumun is hand-illustrated by the same Grade-A Quality Jumbo artists who bring you *Disney's Doug*, the television series.

Disney PRESS

New York

Original characters for "The Funnies" developed by
Jim Jinkins and Joe Aaron.

Printed in the United States of America.

1 3 5 7 9 10 8 6 4 2

The artwork for this book was prepared using pen and ink.

The text for this book is set in 13-point Leewood.

Library of Congress Catalog Card Number: 00-100172

ISBN 0-7868-4410-8

For more Disney Press fun, visit www.disneybooks.com

CONTENTS

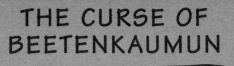

THE CURSE OF BEETENKAUMUN

The students of the Beebe Bluff Middle School held their breath as they prepared to enter the band room. The music stands had all been taken out to make room for the greatest exhibit ever to visit Bluffington. Principal Bob White, who had arranged for the exhibit, stood in the middle of the room welcoming the students. "Young persons, today is a day you will remember for the rest of your life," he said. "Today I, your mayor—I mean, your principal, have brought to you this amazing relic to prove how cultured and tasty I am. Meet King Beetenkaumun, fresh from ruling the Beetentonian Desert. He's a mummy, not a mayor. Tell your parents to vote for me."

Doug, Patti, Connie, and Skeeter moved slowly up to the big gold mummy-shaped sarcophagus and peeked inside. King Beetenkaumun lay as he had been placed 5,000 years before, wrapped in thousands of tiny ancient Band-Aids.

The four friends took a last look and quietly filed into the hall.

Skeeter broke into a dance, imitating the movements of the ancient Beetgyptians on the sides of the mummy case and started singing. "Now when I die, this would be really neat. Don't want no fancy funeral. Just one like Old King Beet!"

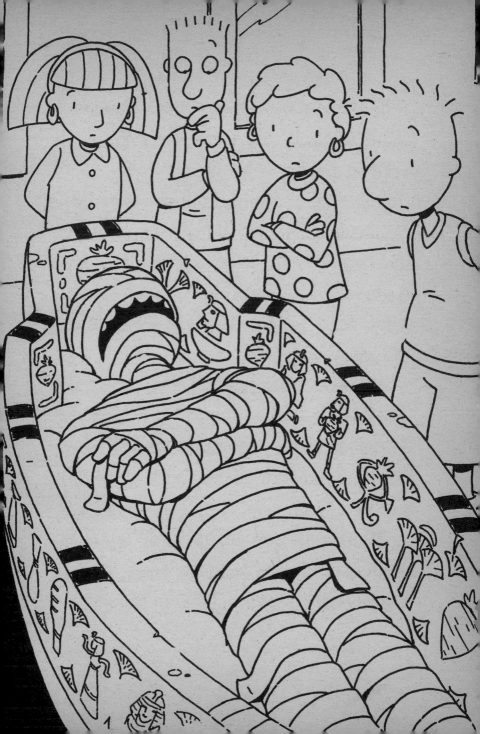

Connie shuddered. "It's creepy to think of a person inside all those bandages sitting in our band room," she said.

"Don't worry," Doug said. "It's just an old mummy. It can't hurt anybody."

"That's what you think!" Roger Klotz said behind them. They all turned to face Roger and his gang: the principal's son, Willy White; Ned Cauphee; and thick-headed Boomer Bledsoe.

"What do you mean, Roger?" Patti asked.

"Well, everybody knows about the Curse of Beetenkaumun," Roger said. "That mummy brings bad luck wherever it goes."

"He's right. I've heard strange things about that mummy," Connie said excitedly.

"You don't really believe in curses, do

you?" said Doug. "They don't make much sense."

"Whatever you say, Funnie Face," Roger replied. "You'll change your mind if that curse kicks in. Of course, I won't have to worry." Roger motioned to Ned, who pulled a spray can out of his pocket. It slipped out of his fingers and fell to the floor, where Roger snatched it up.

"What's that?" asked Doug.

"It's Klotz's Save-You-From-the-Curse Mummy Repellent," said Roger. "This is going to make me more famous than the flood named Roger."

"It's pH-balanced to keep you mummy free," Willy White announced.

"So strong, you can even skip a day," Boomer Bledsoe added.

Doug stared at them. "That's the most ridiculous thing I've ever heard. No one will buy it."

"Not at any price," said Skeeter.

Roger's gang laughed as Doug, Patti, Connie, and Skeeter went off to the cafeteria. They sat down at a table with Beebe Bluff. Everyone was talking about the mummy.

"Well, I think it's wonderful to bring such culture to Bluffington," said Beebe. "His gold-and-jewel-encrusted sarcophagus would really look good in my room. I could keep my shoes in it."

Patti spoke up. "My dad wrote a paper about the Beetgyptians. I brought a copy of one of the scrolls with me. It's got a story about King Beetenkaumun, but it's written in Beet-o-glyphics." Patti reached into her book bag to get the ancient scroll and screamed. When she pulled out her hand a large, iridescent beetle flew out and landed in her pudding. As the beetle struggled to pull itself out of her dessert, the scroll fell open onto the floor.

"Look!" Skeeter honked. "There's pictures of beetles all over the scroll!"

Doug picked up the parchment. He couldn't read Beet-o-glyphics but he knew beetles when he saw them. Patti looked at the manuscript with surprise. "Oh no, Doug! Maybe there *is* a curse!" said Patti. "There are beetles on that scroll about Beetenkaumun and now there's a beetle in the pudding!"

"I'm telling my daddy," Beebe said and ran from the room.

"I'm telling everyone," Connie said.

"I wonder if there's such a thing as an ancient bug exterminator?" Skeeter pondered.

"We're all doomed!" Connie shouted.

As the bell rang to end lunch, Doug

took out his detective's notebook. He did not believe in curses, but there was something strange going on that was upsetting his friends. Doug was going to get to the bottom of the mummy's curse.

Doug and Skeeter talked about the curse on their way back to the locker room after gym class. "I can't believe that beetle could come all the way from the Beetentonian Desert," said Doug.

"I guess you're right," said Skeeter. "After all, Bluffington is a long way from the desert!" But when Skeeter put his foot into his shoes, he froze.

"What is it, Skeeter?" Doug asked. Slowly, Skeeter pulled his foot out of his shoe. Sand spilled onto the floor and stuck to his sock.

"Doug," said Skeeter, "deserts are full of sand, aren't they? So is my shoe. This is really weird. Are you *sure* this isn't a curse?"

Doug stared at the sand for a second and then shook his head vehemently. "It's definitely a clue, but it doesn't mean there's a curse. There has to be a logical explanation. Come on, we promised Patti we'd watch her big beetball game after school."

Doug and Skeeter hurried to Lucky Duck Park. Skeeter kept stopping to shake more sand from his shoe, so the game had already started when they got there. They sat down next to Connie in the bleachers. Doug saw Patti run across the field to catch a grounder. When Patti tried to throw the beetball to the third baseman, it stayed in her hand. The other team scored the winning run while Patti held on to the ball. "What's going on?" honked Skeeter. "Why didn't Patti throw the ball?"

"Help! I'm stuck!" Patti cried. Doug and

his friends jumped off the bleachers and ran onto the field. Patti's beetball was dripping with a mysterious sticky slime.

"It's the mummy's curse!" Connie cried.

"Oh, Doug, what are we going to do?" asked Patti.

Doug pictured himself as Race Canyon, holding a torch as he entered a tomb in the Valley of the Beets. The walls were covered with pictures of beetles, and Patti stuck close to him for protection. Doug held his torch high above his head. "Oh, Doug, you're so tomb raider-y!" Patti said, putting her hand on his shoulder.

"Doug, what are we going to do?" Patti repeated, shaking Doug back to reality. "I'll never play beetball again if the mummy has anything to say about it!"

"Without Patti we'll never win another beetball game," said Skeeter. "This mummy has to be stopped!"

"Patti, we have to go look at that mummy again," Doug said. "There's something funny going on here!"

When Doug, Patti, and Skeeter got back to Beebe Bluff Middle School, there was a line stretching down the hall outside the band room. Everyone in Bluffington wanted to see King Beetenkaumun now that the school was rumored to be cursed.

Principal White stood outside happily handing out campaign buttons that read IF KING BEET COULD TALK, HE'D SAY, "VOTE FOR BOB WHITE!"

Roger was right beside him waving a

spray can and shouting, "Get your own bottle of Klotz's Mummy Curse Repellent here." Just then Boomer Bledsoe walked by. Doug noticed there was something strange about the way he was walking. He kept stopping to scratch himself in

different places. It reminded Doug of something, but he couldn't remember what. "Come on," he said to Skeeter and Patti. "Let's follow him."

As Boomer walked down the hallway, Doug remembered walking the same way when he came back from the beach with sand in his underwear. Doug stopped next to Willy White's locker, noticing a small trail of slime on the outside. "That's the same stuff that was on my beetball!" Patti exclaimed. "Is the mummy after Willy, too, now?"

Doug was looking down the hall. He saw Ned Cauphee leaning over the water fountain. He seemed to be looking down the drain and whistling. "What are you doing?" Doug asked.

Ned spun around and pocketed the jar he had in his hand. "Nothing," he said. "I'm just whistling Beet-ovan's 'Moonlight Sonata' for piano and I got thirsty." With that, Ned walked off. Doug took one more look at the water fountain. As he did, a large shiny beetle crawled up out of the drain.

"This is too weird," said Doug. He pulled out his notebook. "Roger said the curse goes everywhere the mummy goes. Connie backed him up. Patti got a beetle in her book bag. Skeeter got sand in his sneakers. Patti's beetball got slimed. The same slime is on Willy's locker, and Boomer's walking like he's got sand in his underwear. Now Ned is whistling beetles out of water fountains. But I haven't seen the mummy walking around, and he's the one who's supposed to be making all this strange stuff happen. Guys, I think we've solved the Curse of Beetenkaumun."

Doug, Patti, and Skeeter hurried back to the exhibit. Principal White was still handing out buttons and beside him Roger

23

was still trying to get famous by selling his mummy-repellent spray, claiming it would keep anyone from being cursed.

"There is no curse!" announced Doug, walking into the room. "Boomer Bledsoe put sand in Skeeter's shoes and Willy White slimed the beetball. Ned Cauphee hid the beetle in Patti's book bag. Roger and his gang were just trying to scare everyone!"

"No curse?" said Roger. "Of course there's a curse. Why else would I be selling my famous Klotz Mummy Repellent?"

"Because you're a big fat cheater?" Doug retorted.

"Why, I oughta . . ." Roger began, but before he could clobber Doug the now angry crowd clamored around them.

"No curse?" they all cried. "I want my money back for that mummy repellent!" As Roger frantically gave back money to his angry customers, the rest of the crowd pulled off their campaign buttons and

stomped out. Finally the band room was empty except for Principal White, Roger and his gang, Doug, Skeeter, Patti, and King Beet himself.

"I'm glad you young persons like curses," Principal White said to Roger, Boomer, Ned, and Willy. "But you haven't seen anything until you see 5,000 years of detention. Starting right now! And you, Willy. Just wait 'til you get home!"

"I guess you were right about the curse, Doug," said Patti. "King Beet would be proud."

"Yeah, Doug," Skeeter honked. "You really got this case all wrapped up."

FUNKYTOWN

The banner in front of the roller rink at Funkytown read HAVE A GROOVY BIRTHDAY, BEEBE BLUFF! Funkytown was Bluffington's amusement park and tribute to the disco era. As the richest family in town, the Bluffs had rented out the entire rink for their daughter's thirteenth birthday. Doug, Skeeter, Patti, and the rest of their friends from the Beebe Bluff Middle School were all invited to a roller boogie disco party.

"Hi, Dad," Doug said, skating over to his father.

"Don't call me Dad, Doug Baby," Phil said, scratching the fake beard he wore. "Today I'm Funkadelic Funnie, the baddest deejay in Bluffington." His father had explained to Doug that in the 1970s "bad" meant "good."

Phil Funnie flipped through some super-groovy record albums while singing off-key. "You're my disco mama! Uh-huh. Uh-huh." Doug looked around to see if anyone heard. Fortunately, the only other kid near-by was his best human friend, Skeeter, who was making his own weird noises.

Phil growled loudly into the micro-phone. "Listen up all you happening dudes and dudettes, the Funkadelic Funnie's comin' at ya with three funka-delic skate-offs! First, we're gonna have a skate just for the ladies, then one for all you gents. After that we're gonna get groovy with a skate for couples—so all you disco kings go and find yourself a queen and . . . SKATE ON!" Phil put on a song called "Disco Madness."

Doug skated as far away from Funkadelic Funnie as possible. He loved his dad but the other kids were sure to laugh at him, and laugh at Doug, too. Suddenly Beebe Bluff skated over with Patti Mayonnaise. "Doug, I can't believe your father," Beebe said. She wore shiny gold platform boots and an orange off-the-shoulder skating costume trimmed with ostrich feathers.

Doug's face got red. "He's not always like that," he tried to explain.

"Don't be bashful, Doug," Patti said. She looked really pretty in her red shiny shorts and rainbow suspenders and a button that read, NA NU, NA NU. "You're father's the coolest!"

"Huh?" Doug said. Maybe the disco beat was interfering with his hearing. "You think he's cool?"

"Of course he's cool," said Beebe, dropping feathers on the floor. "I wouldn't have anything less at my party!"

Doug smiled broadly. "Yeah, I guess the Funnies are pretty cool," he said.

Beebe and Patti skated to the rink with the other girls. As Patti skated by the SuperFly shake machine, one of her suspenders got caught on a nozzle. Skunky Beaumont, who was sitting beside the machine watching it shake, reached up and unhooked the suspender. "Whoa. Cool slingshot."

"Thanks, Skunky," Patti said. "You're a real gentleman."

Doug sighed as he watched Patti skate away. He wished he could impress her like that. As he listened to the music he imagined himself skating across the rink in a white suit and platform skates six inches high. He spun around on one leg and then struck a pose with one hand on his hip and the other pointed in the air. He heard lightning flash and the crowd said, "Shazzam!"

Doug spotted Patti Mayonnaise in the crowd, her eyes sparkling with delight at his undeniable grooviness. Doug skated

over to her and flashed a smile. "Hey, Patti," Doug said smoothly. "How's about you and me puttin' our wheels together for the couples skate?"

"Sure, Doug," Patti said, smiling. "Why are you talking like that?"

Doug felt his face go beet red. Suddenly he realized that he was talking to Patti in real life, not in his fantasy. He had actually asked her to skate couples with him and—hold on a minute—she had said yes!

"Thanks, Patti," Doug said quickly. "That would be . . . great . . . I mean . . . groovy!"

"See you later," said Patti. She started to skate off, and then turned around. "By the way, it's girls skate now. You should really sit down."

Doug looked around and realized he

was the only boy in the rink. Some of the girls were giggling at him. "I didn't know you were a girl, Doug," giggled Beebe Bluff in her ostrich feathers.

Doug skated out of the rink so quickly that he almost ran into the SuperFly shake machine. As he did, Doug imagined himself skating with Patti during couples skate. There he was, arm in arm with the most beautiful girl in the universe, when he tripped on the laces of his skate and spun out of control, knocking people down right and left. People screamed. Patti gasped. Doug and Patti went flying into the snack bar, flipped over the counter, and landed in a big vat of Tab soda, which Phil had explained was very popular in the '70s.

Doug shook his head to clear away the horrible image. "I need a SuperFly shake," he said. "I need a good protein base if I'm going to skate with Patti." Doug sat down on a bench next to his mother, Theda, who was with his little sister, Dirtbike. He took off his skates and left them on the bench next to his mother before he went to the snack bar.

Doug ordered the extra-beetified Super-Fly shake with rainbow-colored pop rocks that exploded in your mouth. After listening to it crackle he felt much better about his skate with destiny. "Maybe Patti will want to keep skating with me after the contest," he said. "And then we could—" Doug broke off as he caught a glimpse of Patti. She was smiling and laughing, and talking to . . . Guy Graham! Guy was the editor of *The Weekly Beebe* and he was in eighth grade. And Doug suspected that he liked Patti . . . a lot. "Oh, no!" he said, hurrying back through the crowd to the bench where he had left his skates. "I've got to get ready for my skate with Patti!" But when Doug got to the bench, only his right skate was sitting there. "Where's my other skate?" Doug cried, looking all around for his left skate. "I can't skate with Patti on one foot! I'll be a loser! I'll be a turkey! Aw, man!"

Doug got on all fours and squeezed under the bench. He found a piece of chewed gum, three nickels, an old movie ticket, and a pet rock. He didn't see his skate anywhere. "A skate can't just vanish," Doug said. "Someone has to take it. But who?"

Doug looked across Funkytown, which was now filled with suspects. He remembered his detective's notebook in the back pocket of his white polyester bell-bottoms. Right in front of him, Skeeter tripped over his wide bell-bottom cuffs and slid across the polished floor. The sliding sound was immediately followed by mean laughter that could only belong to Roger Klotz, Bluffington's least favorite bully.

"Loser!" Roger called as he skated past Skeeter. Then he looked up at Doug. "Valentine's almost as big a loser as you, Funnie!"

Doug was about to ignore Roger's

insult as one of many, but then he remembered his missing skate. "Ruining my life
is Roger's favorite hobby," Doug said,
writing his name down in his notebook.
"He could have watched me go to get my
SuperFly shake, told my mom I was in an
accident, and then stolen my skate. It
must have been Roger!"

But just then Guy Graham skated past.
Doug remembered that Guy had been
talking to Patti earlier. "Hi, Doug," he said
with a toothy smile. He snapped his fingers. "Nice suit!"

"Nice suit?" Doug repeated as Guy
skated away. "What did that mean?"
Suddenly Doug began to suspect that Guy
was hiding something. "I'll bet he was
asking Patti to skate couples when he

talked to her before. She must have told him she was skating with me. Guy could have hijacked my skate so that he and Patti could go together."

Doug imagined Guy, dressed all in black, attached to the ceiling by a cable. Guy probably lowered himself inch by inch until he was suspended just above the bench. When Theda turned away, Guy picked up the skate in his teeth and then rewound the cable back up to the ceiling and disappeared. "Very clever," said Doug, making a note in his detective's notebook. Doug now had two suspects. He couldn't think of anyone else with the motive and opportunity. That is, until Skunky Beaumont rolled past him. "Gloamin'," said Skunky, as he squatted down into a

cannonball. He was going in the opposite direction from all the other boys, but he didn't seem to notice. Or did he?

Doug suddenly remembered Patti's sweet smile when she thanked Skunky for helping her when she was stuck on the SuperFly shake machine. How could any boy not want to skate couples with Patti after they'd been smiled at like that? Doug imagined Skunky skating up to Patti just after girls skate. "Whoa, dudette. You. Me. Let's roll."

To Doug's horror, Patti replied, "Oh, Skunky, you're so . . . way cool, man. That would be, like, totally . . . you know!"

With Patti's consent, Skunky did a back flip out of the rink and cartwheeled over to the bench. He picked up the skate and then flipped hand over feet into the locker room. "Totally," sighed Patti, watching him go.

Doug was so upset he didn't even make a note in his detective's notebook. "I guess I'll never get to skate with Patti," he said, as "Boogie Shoes"—the music for the couples-only skate—started to play.

"Ready, Doug?" Patti said, skating over to him.

"Patti, I . . ." suddenly Doug heard a noise beside him like a little engine revving up, followed by a giggle. "Wait a minute!" said Doug.

"I left my skate with Mom when I went to get my shake," Doug said to himself.

"Roger could have taken it . . . because he's Roger. Guy could have taken it because he was consumed with jealousy. Skunky might have taken it to impress Patti—and it might have worked. So who took my skate?"

The engine-revving noise got louder and something bumped Doug's leg. "Dirtbike!" he cried, looking down.

Doug's little sister was riding her new souped-up baby Big Wheel. Dirtbike was sitting on the toe end of Doug's missing white platform skate, holding on to the

laces at the top and pushing herself along with her feet. "Br-r-r-r! Br-r-r-r-r!" drooled Dirtbike, revving her "engine."

"Dirtbike, you're the most!" Doug said, impressed with his little sister's grooviness. He picked her up and Patti applauded.

"Oh, Doug!" said Patti as he slipped on his skate. "Let's take her with us!"

Doug and Patti and Dirtbike hit the floor together. Doug and Patti each held one of Dirtbike's hands and Dirtbike put one foot on Doug's left skate and the other on Patti's right skate. Doug and Patti sang, "I'm gonna put on my my my my my boogie shoes, and boogie with you."

"Br-r-r-! Br-r-r-r-!" answered Dirtbike, very pleased with her double Big Wheel.

In the center of the rink, Beebe Bluff

and Skeeter Valentine joined hands and leaned backward, spinning around in a dizzy circle. Beebe's ostrich feathers flew up like a small tornado and Skeeter honked them away.

As the music faded, Wolfman Funnie let out his last howl of the evening. "First place for the couples skate goes to the birthday chick—that's Beebe Bluff—and her partner, Skeeter Valentine!" Doug's best human friend, Skeeter, honked a victory cheer as he and Beebe skated up to claim their trophy.

"And a special prize goes to our superbad trio—Doug, Patti, and the Boogie Baby!" Doug and Patti skated up to Phil and got their trophy. Dirtbike climbed inside, and they held it above their heads.

"Keep on truckin'," said Doug. "Disco lives forever!"

Beebe stepped up to the microphone. "This birthday was the baddest," she announced, "and by the baddest, I mean the coolest!"

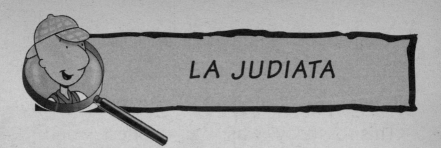

LA JUDIATA

Theda Funnie fell to one knee and raised her arms up to the heavens. "I thought I was living, but I was only breathing. How could I live without Judy?"

Phil Funnie stood behind her. "I ate and I slept, but what was the point? Oh, how could I live without Judy?"

Phil and Theda clasped each other's hands and sang in a heart-wrenching duet. "And then she came, she made it all worthwhile, our treasure, our star, our beautiful child. We didn't live until Judy. We never lived until Judy!"

"Cut!" cried Judy, walking out from the den into the living room. "Mom, you've got to show more emotion on that line. Can't you remember how awful your life was before I was born?"

"Well, dear, I did enjoy high school and college. And your father and I used to travel—"

"But, Mom!" Judy cut in. "You don't understand—this is drama!"

"Oh, brother!" sighed Doug. "Judy's really gone over the edge this time!"

Judy was under a lot of stress. Since being awarded a grant from the Vole School of Emoting to produce *La Judiata*, an opera based on her life, Doug's sister had thought of nothing but the performance. The opera was as yet unfinished, but Judy had entered it in a competition for "Obsessively Perfectionistic but Still More Talented Than You'll Ever Be" artists. The winner of the competition would win a trip to the Divas Spa for Forgetting How Annoying the Rest of the World Is. The contest meant a lot to Judy, so the Funnies had agreed to play themselves in a performance at the Moody Theater, which was part of Judy's school.

Judy had rehearsed them mercilessly all week while still trying to finish the all important ending number, "No Judy, No Nothing." She had rewritten it six times, but it still wasn't right. "Doug, the closing number is my most important moment," she had explained to him. "It's where I sum up all my hopes, my dreams, my struggles to overcome the ordinary family I was born into. It has to be perfect!"

"But Judy, if the show is about our family, then why is it all about you?" Doug asked. Judy sighed and shook her head.

"Because I'm the only Funnie who can rivet the attention of an audience for a whole evening."

As Judy continued to mold her weary parents into the operatic sensations she wished they were, Doug and his dog Porkchop looked over his solo: "How can one boy compare . . . to Judy."

"I don't know about this, Porkchop," Doug said. "I can't see sitting through a whole evening of how great Judy is." Porkchop nodded and rolled over on the floor.

Leaving her parents alone for a moment, Judy turned on a tape recording of "O Judy Mio," which would be lip-synched by her little sister, Cleopatra Dirtbike. As soon as the music began to play, Cleopatra sat up and gurgled happily. "That's it!" Judy cried, clasping her hands over her heart. "It's perfect. Listen, listen all of you! There is perhaps one Funnie who shares my artistic soul!"

Doug and Porkchop lay on the floor and groaned.

On the afternoon of the show, Judy locked herself in her room to finish the closing number. Doug practiced his solo in front of his mirror. "Anything I can do, she can do better. She can do anything better than me," he sang reluctantly. "Oh, how can one boy compare . . . to Judy?" Porkchop shook his head and left the room.

Doug finished his song and then lay down on his bed. He really wasn't looking forward to singing it in front of a roomful of people with artistic temperaments like his sister, who yelled at him whenever he made a mistake. Doug imagined himself walking out onto a stage dressed in a tuxedo. The crowd gasped. Doug bowed graciously, thinking they were overcome by his stage presence. He began to sing. "Hey," someone in the audience yelled. "Where's your pants?"

Doug was confused. "What? I'm wearing my pants." He looked down. "Oh, my mistake. I'm not wearing my pants." Doug looked around the stage for something to hide his bare legs, but the only other thing on stage was a skinny microphone stand. No matter how he stood behind it, he stuck out on all sides.

"Where's your pants? Where's your pants?" the whole audience chanted, stamping their feet. Meanwhile, Judy hissed to him from offstage. "Doug, you're ruining my show. Doug! Doug!"

Doug snapped to attention in his room. He was in front of his mirror again, fully dressed, and Judy was yelling. "Doug!" she shrieked. "You're in big trouble!"

"What else is new?" mumbled Doug as he went out into the hall. Judy was wild-eyed, even more so than usual. Doug took a step back.

"Where's my song?" she demanded.

"Anything I can do, she can do better . . ." Doug began on cue. Judy held up her hand dramatically.

"That's not the song I meant!" she cried. "Although, if it was, you were flat. I'm talking about my grand finale that I finally finished: 'No Judy, No Nothing.' I went to the kitchen for some sparkling beet juice to celebrate the completion of my immortal opus. When I came back to my room it was gone!"

Doug looked confused. Judy flung her hand to her forehead and turned away. "Oh, Doug, how could you?" she cried. "Couldn't you have held your all-consuming jealousy of me in check just this once? Did you have to steal my greatest work to prevent me from achieving my long-deserved triumph? A triumph in which you can't share, being only Doug. Oh, Doug, for shame! For shame, Doug!"

About halfway through Judy's speech, Doug had pulled out his detective's notebook and begun trying to solve the case of the missing aria. It was his most important case to date. He had to solve it to clear his name and possibly preserve his life. Forgetting his pants was nothing compared to the wrath of Judy if he didn't find that song. "If you don't bring my song to me by the time we have to leave for the theater," Judy said, "the Funnie family will have one less cast member. Do I make myself clear, little brother?" Before Doug could answer, Judy marched back into her room and slammed the door to begin her preperformance meditation.

"The best place to begin my investigation," Doug said, "would be to search Judy's room." From behind the closed door, Doug could hear Judy begin chanting her mantra: "I'm a star . . . I'm a star . . . I'm a star . . ."

"But I can't go in there with Judy in there," Doug said, "so I'll have to question the rest of the cast—er, family—as to when they last saw the song. That's what a detective would do."

Doug knew that Judy had sent his parents into the den to do vocal exercises. He found them lying on the couch drinking Long Island Beet Teas with cold washcloths over their eyes. The Beet Biscuit

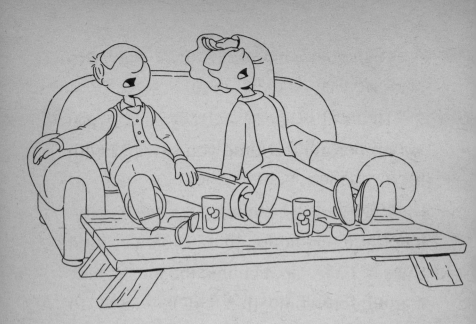

Flower Hour played on the TV. When they heard the door open, Phil and Theda sat up and started singing. "Mi, Mi, Mi," they sang. "Oh, it's you, Doug." His parents dropped back onto the couch.

"Mom, Dad, we have a problem," said Doug. "Someone has taken Judy's closing number."

"Oh, no," said Phil. "'No Judy, No Nothing'?"

"That's the one," said Doug. "Do you remember the last time you saw her with it?"

Phil and Theda thought for a moment. "We were rehearsing that last verse," said Theda. "I fell a beat behind the music. Judy started screaming that I didn't have an artist's soul. Then she picked up the song and stomped out."

"Wait," said Phil. "First she said that either talent skipped a generation in our family, or we had taken the wrong baby home from the hospital. Then she picked up the song and stomped out."

Doug made a note in his detective's notebook and left his parents to their nap.

"I don't think they did it," he said. "Judy's had them rehearsing in the den all day, so they couldn't have taken the song."

Doug went into the living room to question Dirtbike, who was sitting in her playpen. She couldn't have taken it but maybe she knew something. "Dirtbike," said Doug. "Do you remember what Judy was doing the last time you saw her?"

Dirtbike smiled at Doug. She put her finger in her mouth and sucked on it for a second. Then she opened her mouth and screamed. She beat her fists in the air and wailed to the heavens. Then she collapsed back into the playpen, flinging one chubby hand to her forehead. Except for wearing a diaper, she looked exactly like Judy.

"Thank you, Dirtbike," Doug said, tick-

ling the baby. Judy was right. Dirtbike had talent. That was the best Judy imitation he'd ever seen.

"But that still doesn't tell me who took the song," Doug said. There was only one more family member that Doug hadn't interrogated. He opened the back door and headed out to Porkchop's tepee. As he neared it, he heard music being played on an electric keyboard. "Whoever took Judy's song did it this afternoon, right after she finished it. Mom and Dad were in the den, Dirtbike was in her playpen. I was in my room. Judy went to the kitchen for sparkling beet juice. That only leaves one more suspect."

Doug stepped into the tepee just as Porkchop finished up a riff on his electric keyboard. Doug immediately recognized Judy's song, although something sounded different. "Porkchop, you took the song? Come on! We're in big trouble!"

Porkchop smiled sheepishly at Doug and handed him the music for the closing number.

"Doug!" Theda called. "It's time to go to the show!"

Doug took the music and ran back to the house. The audience was already beginning to arrive when they got to the Moody Theater, so he just had time to slip the song under the door of Judy's dressing room before getting dressed for the show. He remembered his pants.

The opera was a big hit, especially the closing number: "No one person makes a family . . . not even Judy." Judy looked a little surprised as she sang it. It was almost as if she didn't remember writing the words at all. "My family's nothing without me . . . but I'm nothing without them. No one person makes a family, even if they're Judy!"

Doug and his parents looked at each other, surprised. "Wow," Phil said. "The tune's the same but the words are really different from the last time I heard her practicing. I can't believe Judy is writing such nice things about us!"

"Yes," agreed Theda. "Our little girl's becoming so grown-up!" she sniffed, tears in her eyes.

Later, over beet juice and crudités, Judy

answered questions about the opera. "I wrote most of it in a fit of artistic frenzy," she said. "The finale really wrote itself. I don't even remember writing such poetry. I must have entered some kind of fugue state of intense creativity."

Porkchop made a "hmm" noise. Doug looked at him. "So *that's* why you took her music!" he said.

Porkchop picked up Doug's detective's notebook and winked. Doug thought he seemed to be congratulating him on a case well-solved.

All the Funnies celebrated with beet split sundaes when they got home. "We Funnies are really something when we all work together," Phil said.

"Speaking of working together," said Doug. "The finale turned out really well, didn't it?"

Judy smiled and looked down at her sundae. "Yes, it did," she said. "I was wrong to think I had to do it all myself when I have a family as great as this one to help me out. Thanks for helping me even if I didn't know I needed it."

"No problem," said Doug, winking at Porkchop. "We'll always be here to remind you that you need us."

A HARD BEET'S NIGHT

"I've never seen so many people in Lucky Duck Park!" Doug said, looking around. Skeeter and Patti nodded in awe.

"I can't believe we're going to be in a movie," Skeeter said. "And we get to see the Beets, too!"

The Beets were filming a concert movie, *A Hard Beet's Night*, in Lucky Duck Park. All of Bluffington had turned out to be extras. As they entered the park, Doug saw Roger Klotz walking by carrying a big duffel bag. Something hot pink with leopard spots trailed out of one side of it.

"Hey, Roger," Doug said, "aren't you going to watch the Beets and be in the movie?"

Roger sneered. "Nobody's following those Beets anymore," he said. "They're so beat they're flat. There's a new sound in town and soon everyone will know it. Even a loser like you, Funnie!"

Doug couldn't believe it. The Beets had been his favorite band since he moved to Bluffington the year before. "The Beets can't be beat," he insisted loyally. Roger laughed and went on his way.

"Doug," Patti said, tugging his sleeve. "Let's get a spot right up at the front."

"I want to make sure they get my best side in the movie," Skeeter honked, showing Doug and Patti the difference between his two sides. They couldn't see it, but they moved toward the stage anyway.

As they neared the front, Connie Benge pushed past them in a hurry. "Sorry," she said breathlessly, "I just have to get to the stage."

Doug wasn't surprised that Connie was so excited. She played the electric guitar and could rock with the greatest of rockers. "Do you want to sit with us, Connie?" Patti asked.

Connie hesitated. "Thanks, but I can't. I've . . . uh . . . I've got someone waiting for me. See you later. It's going to be a great show. Really great!" Connie hurried away and disappeared into the crowd.

Just as the show was about to begin,

Chap Lipman, the Beets' drummer, appeared on stage. He looked upset. "We're ever so sorry," he said to the crowd. "But we seem to have run into a spot of trouble. Somebody's nicked our guitar player. Have any of you chaps seen Munroe?"

Doug gasped. Without Munroe Yoder, the Beets couldn't play a beat. "What are they going to do?" asked Doug.

"Doug, you should get on the case!" Skeeter said. "You're a detective!"

"Ummm, I don't think I can solve this," Doug said. "Munroe Yoder's a rock star. How could I ever find him?"

"Oh, Doug, I'll bet you could. You could find anything!" For a moment Doug imagined himself meeting with

Patti under a lamppost in Lucky Duck Park. "Miss Mayonnaise, I've found your rock star," Doug said casually, while flipping a coin.

"Oh, Doug, you're so investigator-y!" said Patti.

"Maybe I can find out what happened to Munroe," Doug said, coming out of his fantasy and pulling out his detective's notebook. "I guess there's no harm in trying."

"Yeah, it's not like you could make him more lost," Skeeter agreed.

Doug opened his notebook and wrote down, Lost: One Beet, Munroe Yoder, guitar player, English. Distinguishing marks: cool pirate bandanna, awesome boots, excellent sunglasses, carrying electric guitar. "Let's go," said Doug, signaling to his friends. "We have to question the band. That's proper detective procedure."

Doug found the Beets backstage in a state of confusion. "It's my fault!" Chap Lipman was crying. "I ate the last of the Marmite!" He held up a jar with brown sticky stuff at the bottom. Doug nodded and made a note: Subject has questionable taste in food.

"No, it's my fault!" Wendy Nespah insisted. "I borrowed his wellies and I got them all muddy."

"Well, well, well. May I see the wellies?" Doug asked. Wendy held up a pair of rubber boots. Doug made a note: Subject lacks all-weather foot protection. The group's bassist, Flounder, stared at

Munroe's empty chair, sadly plucking out a tune on his bass.

"This is serious," Skeeter said softly to Patti and Doug.

"When was the last time Munroe was seen?" Doug asked. The Beets thought about it.

"We all played cricket this morning," Flounder remembered.

"And then we sang 'God Save the Queen,'" said Chap.

"And the Queen Mum, too!" said Wendy. "Then Munroe went into his trailer!"

"Let's go," said Doug. Patti led the way back to Munroe's trailer and the Beets stood by as Flounder unlocked the door. The first thing Doug noticed in Munroe's trailer was the needlepoint. It was everywhere:

on pillows, hanging on the wall—even decorative doorknob warmers.

"Munroe always does needlepoint before we go on," Wendy explained. "It's brilliant for his nerves."

"Confidentially, he gets terrible stage fright," said Chap. "Without the needlepoint he's a right mess on stage."

Wendy picked up a piece of unfinished work and held it up for Doug. It was a tea cozy with needlepoint pictures of all the Beets on it. "He was working on this before he popped out," she said, wiping a tear. Wendy read out the words on the tea cozy. "To Mum. When you have a spot of tea, think of your lad across the sea. Luv, Munroe."

Doug scribbled in his notebook:

82

Subject does needlepoint, also loves tea-drinking mother. "What does Munroe usually do next?"

Chap Lipman held up his drumsticks and pointed to the tuning knobs. "Next he's got to tune his guitar, hasn't he?" he said. "Can't go on stage without the proper Beet sound."

Doug looked at all his notes. "We know everyone else in Bluffington is out in Lucky Duck Park except for Roger, who went somewhere carrying a pink leopard skin. We know that Munroe played cricket this morning, and sang 'God Save the Queen.' He did his needlepoint and tuned his guitar. But where is he?"

Patti jumped in. "What is the very last thing Munroe does before you go on stage?" she asked the other Beets.

The Beets were silent for a moment, then they all answered together. "The Portoloo!" they cried, rushing outside.

"But where's it gone?" Wendy said, looking all around. "I'm quite sure there was a Portoloo right here this morning. Now there's only this group of palm trees."

"Palm trees?" Doug said. "In Lucky Duck Park? Something tells me that's a clue." As Doug neared the palm trees, he could hear guitar music coming from behind the fronds, and a voice singing.

"Help, I'm in the loo! Help, I'm talking to you! Help, you know it's dark in here. Heeeeeeeeeeeeeeeellllllllllllllllppppppppppp!"

"That's Monroe all right!" Chap Lipman exclaimed. "Where are you, lad?"

Doug and Skeeter pushed aside the palm trees, which were potted, not attached to the ground. "Someone put these here to camouflage the Portoloo," Chap said.

"Someone who didn't want the Beets to play," said Doug, walking right up to the Portoloo.

"That sounds pretty good, Munroe," Wendy called, knocking on the door.

"Sit tight, old chap," Chap Lipman added as he unlocked the Portoloo door. "We'll have you out of this in no time!"

Munroe blinked and stepped out into the sunshine. "What happened?" asked Doug.

"It's rather odd, actually," Munroe said. "I heard the door just shut behind me.

Thought I heard someone outside. When I looked through the keyhole I saw a chap with red hair and a wigged-out chick with hot-pink leopard spots!"

Just then everyone heard someone jamming on an electric guitar. If Doug didn't know better, he would have thought it was Munroe himself. The Beets rushed back to the stage with Patti, Doug, and Skeeter right behind them.

"Look at that!" Flounder said, pointing to the scene on stage. "She's the beetest!"

Connie Benge was onstage. She was doing a blistering guitar solo and the crowd, thinking this was part of the Beets' show, was going wild. Doug's dog, Porkchop, was right in the front row, hip-hopping to the music.

"I told you," said Roger, coming up beside Doug. Roger was wearing a T-shirt that said CONNIE BENGE: UNBEETABLE. "I knew once the crowd heard Connie, she'd unseat the Beets!"

Connie sure was wowing the crowd, and the Beets thought it was great. In a heartbeat the Beets had joined her onstage with their instruments. The crowd roared and starting chanting, "Beets! Beets! Beets!"

"I can't believe it," said Roger. "Why does anyone want to see them when Connie's onstage?"

"Because the Beets can't be beat," Patti informed him.

Onstage, Connie was thrilled to be jamming with her idols, but Roger wasn't happy at all. He wanted this to be Connie's show that he could take credit for. Flounder called Porkchop up onto the stage to dance. "Wait a second!" Roger said to Doug. "My client works alone! That dog isn't under contract! And neither are those Beets!"

Doug smiled and closed his notebook. "Give it up, Roger," he said. "When you're beat, you're beat."

Satisfy your hunger for a good mystery

Check out all of these titles for your own Doug Funnie Mystery Feast!

The Funnie Mysteries #1:
Invasion of the Judy Snatchers
(0-7868-4382-9)

The Funnie Mysteries #3:
The Case of the Baffling Beast
(0-7868-4384-5)

DEVOUR
THEM
ALL!

The Funnie Mysteries #2:
True Graffiti
(0-7868-4383-7)

The Funnie Mysteries #4:
The Curse of Beetenkaumun
(0-7868-4410-8)